Kenya

Tanzania

Lake Natron

Olduvai Gorge

Ngorongoro Conservation Area

Ngorongoro Crater

Lake Magadi

Lake Eyasi

Lake Manyara

Welcome to your adventure!

STOP! Read this first!

Welcome to an action-packed adventure in which you take the starring role!

You're about to enter the Ngorongoro Crater in Tanzania, breathtakingly beautiful and teeming with dangerous African wildlife. On each page choose from different options – according to your instincts, knowledge and intelligence – and make your own path across the crater to safety.

You decide . . .

- How to escape a charging bull elephant
- What to do when you come face to face with a deadly snake
- How to understand monkey alarm calls

. . . and many more life-or-death dilemmas. Along the way you'll discover the facts you need to help you survive.

It's time to test your survival skills – or die trying!

Your adventure starts on page 7.

LOST
IN THE CRATER OF FEAR

TRACEY TURNER

BLOOMSBURY
LONDON OXFORD NEW YORK NEW DELHI SYDNEY

LOST

IN THE CRATER OF FEAR

WARNING!

The instructions in this book are for extreme survival situations only. Always proceed with caution, and ask an adult to supervise – or ideally, seek professional help. If in doubt, consult a responsible adult.

Published 2016 by Bloomsbury Publishing Plc
50 Bedford Square, London, WC1B 3DP

www.bloomsbury.com

978-1-4729-1544-3

Bloomsbury is a registered trademark of Bloomsbury Publishing Plc

Copyright © 2016 Bloomsbury Publishing Plc
Text copyright © 2016 Tracey Turner
Illustration copyright © 2016 Nelson Evergreen
Additional illustrations © Shutterstock

The rights of Tracey Turner and Nelson Evergreen to be identified as the author and illustrator of this work have been asserted by them in accordance with the Copyrights, Designs and Patents Act 1988.

A CIP catalogue for this book is available from the British Library.

All rights reserved. No part of this publication may be reproduced in any form or by any means – graphic, electronic or mechanical, including photocopying, recording, taping or information storage and retrieval systems – without prior permission in writing of the publisher.

Printed and bound by CPI Group (UK) Ltd, Croydon CR0 4YY

The author and publisher accept no responsibility for any accidents that occur as a result of this book

1 3 5 7 9 10 8 6 4 2

You've taken a moment to be by yourself while the rest of your group crowds around the jeep, listening to the guide's lion-attack story. Their voices fade into the background as you look across the crater. It shimmers in the early morning haze. Standing in the middle of the crater, you can see some zebra in the distance, and far beyond them the crater's rim looks green and lush.

The roar of an engine brings you out of your daydream. You turn and see that the jeep is driving away! You call out as loudly as you can, but it's no good. The engine drowns you out. All you can see now is just a far-away cloud of dust as the jeep speeds away. Your heart pounds violently as you realise what's happened.

This African trip was the prize for winning a national schools competition, and you're here with a group of 25 other prize-winners that you haven't really got to know yet. Today, the friend you're teamed with wasn't well and had to stay at the campsite. Without her to raise the alarm, everyone else must have forgotten you. Maybe the guide thought that you'd stayed behind too.

A long, low roar echoes across the crater, chilling your blood. You are completely lost, and, for the moment at least, alone.

With no other options, you shoulder your backpack and set off in the direction the jeep headed.

How will you survive?

Turn to page 8 to find information you need to help you survive.

You are stranded in the Ngorongoro Crater in Tanzania, East Africa. The crater covers about 300 square kilometres, and is part of the 8,300-square-kilometre Ngorongoro Conservation Area. This includes plains, ravines, lakes, forests, and highlands on the western edge of the Great Rift Valley.

Explosive Past

The Ngorongoro Crater is what's left of a huge volcano that erupted 2.5 million years ago. The enormous explosion left a 600 metre deep crater (actually a caldera, a collapsed volcano's cone) 19 kilometres across, which is now the biggest unbroken and unflooded caldera in the world. Its rich grassland and water sources attract many different creatures.

Crater Animals

The crater's grassland, swamps, forests and freshwater make it home to between 25,000 and 30,000 large mammals. Grazing animals include wildebeest, zebra, gazelle, buffalo, warthogs, hippos, rare black rhinos, and elephants. Ostriches stalk the plains, flamingos swoop in to visit the alkaline Lake Magadi, and eagles, vultures, buzzards, and hawks circle above the crater. The crater also contains the highest concentration of predatory animals in Africa. There are lions, cheetahs, hyenas, jackals, and leopards. Needless to say, all of the meat-eating animals, and some of the plant-eating ones, can be very dangerous.

Wildlife Watching

All of this amazing wildlife attracts another kind of animal: human beings. People come to the Ngorongoro Crater for safaris, especially since it's one of the few places in the world where endangered black rhinos breed. The number of safari vehicles is strictly limited, and they have to leave the crater by six o'clock in the evening, giving the animals the night to themselves. The dry season, from June to October, is the most popular time for visitors to the crater.

Ngorongoro People

The Maasai people live in the Ngorongoro Conservation Area. They manage herds of cattle, sheep and goats, and move with their herds in search of grass and water. The Maasai also live in other parts of northern Tanzania and across the border in Kenya (see page 117 for more information on the Maasai).

Turn to page 10.

Crater Survival Tips

- You have come to the Ngorongoro Crater in October, which is a warm time of year but perhaps not as hot as you might think, especially in the early morning. The floor of the crater is much warmer than the sides. Luckily, you're wearing good walking boots and lightweight layers of clothing, which you can take off and put into your backpack as you warm up.
- It's also lucky that you have a two-litre bottle of drinking water in your backpack. Because you are in such a dangerous territory, finding water isn't a priority – it's more important for you to get out before nightfall!
- As you're probably aware, there are animals in the crater that can easily kill you. Approach any animal with caution, even if you don't think it's dangerous, and always keep your distance.
- A predator is more likely to see you as prey if you're running away from it. Its likely response will be to chase you.
- Large carnivores aren't your only worry: look out for smaller dangerous creatures too, and remember that some plant-eating animals can kill people.
- You will have to find a way to stop yourself from panicking. You are in an extremely dangerous situation, but panicking will lead you to make bad decisions. It's possible to survive if you're thinking clearly – with a bit of luck!

Turn to page 11.

You stop walking to stare out across the crater, doing your best to shake off a feeling of impending doom. You know there are campsites at the crater's edge – you're staying in one – but where are they exactly? And how many dangerous animals might be lurking between here and your destination?

You gulp, and force yourself to stop panicking. You tell yourself that the Ngorongoro Crater is a popular tourist attraction, and you probably won't be alone for long.

You have to set off towards the crater's edge. It looks as though you're almost right in the middle, so whichever way you go will be about the same distance to the edge. You decide to walk away from the rising sun, so that it doesn't get in your eyes and blind you to potential danger.

If you decide to walk westwards, go to page 21.

If you decide to walk to the southwest, go to page 18.

Suddenly you hear a strange grunting, snorting sound. What could it be? At least it doesn't sound like the roar of a big cat . . .

An enormous hippo comes lumbering out of the undergrowth. It's not too close to you at the moment, probably heading for the swamp to your left.

Hippos are vegetarians and the animal looks harmless enough. Should you be worried about it?

If you decide to head in the opposite direction from the animal, go to page 21.

If you decide to keep going, go to page 36.

You take off your shirt and raise it up behind your head like a sail to make yourself look bigger. The lion doesn't move. It doesn't look as though it's about to pounce but it's not backing off, either.

Your heart is pounding. You don't think you've ever been this scared in your life! You force down your panic, and try to remember what you read about scaring off predators. You think you remember reading somewhere that talking in a loud but calm voice might confuse a predator enough for it to disregard you as prey.

Licking your dry lips, you tell the lion to back off as loudly and calmly as you can. The animal takes a pace back. Feeling a bit more confident, you tell the lion you're sure there are some tasty gazelle very close by, your voice sounding a hundred times calmer than you're feeling.

To your enormous relief, the lion slinks back into the grass, and lopes off. Thank goodness it was hunting alone.

Go to page 68.

Your eyes are on the horizon, scanning the crater edge for signs of a campsite, when a rustling sound makes you look at the ground in front of you. A long, brown snake whips into view, moving lightning-fast. It stops a couple of metres in front of you – it must be longer than you are tall! You have no idea what kind of snake this is, but you do know that there are dangerous ones in Tanzania.

The snake stares at you, motionless. You gulp. You're not sure what to do. Will it slither away if you chase and shout at it? Is it more likely to attack if you run away?

If you decide to shoo the snake away, go to page 26.

If you choose to run away, go to page 20.

Tanzania's Most Dangerous Snakes

Below are the most dangerous snakes that live in Tanzania. The continent of Africa is home to even more.

- The puff adder kills more people in Africa than any other type of snake, making it the continent's deadliest snake. They can grow to about a metre long and are quite thick.
- The Gaboon viper injects the most venom in one bite of any snake in the world. There are snakes with much more powerful venom, but even so, one bite from the Gaboon viper can kill an adult human being. The snakes, which can measure up to 1.5 metres long, aren't aggressive and rarely bite, however. They live in forests in central and western Africa.
- The boomslang is a highly venomous tree snake found in Africa south of the Sahara Desert. Males are light green while the females are brown. On average they measure 1.5 metres long.
- The black mamba is one of Africa's most feared snakes, and can be aggressive when it feels threatened. It's also huge, measuring up to 2.5 metres long on average. Despite the name, black mambas are brown or olive in colour.

You turn away from the swamp and walk through grassland dotted with trees. Your decision to leave the swamp was probably a wise one because that's where you're most likely to spot a hippo or an elephant. Both would be wonderful sights from the safety of a jeep, but not when you're on foot and completely alone. Hippos and elephants can be very aggressive animals.

Go to page 21.

You spot a herd of gazelle with long, spiral horns, and you remember the guide telling you that these are Thomson's gazelle, the most common kind in Africa. As you pass by them, a couple of the animals turn to stare at you, freeze for a moment, and then go back to munching grass.

Should you keep away from the gazelle? After all, they are prey animals, and there might be hungry predators close by hunting them. On the other hand, if the predators are hunting the gazelle, they might be less likely to pay attention to you.

If you decide to keep your distance from the gazelle, go to page 39.

If you decide to keep walking alongside them, go to page 68.

You walk on, trying not to panic or dwell too much on the variety of large, carnivorous animals that could be prowling nearby.

In the distance you spot a few zebra, and as you draw closer you see that there is actually a large herd of them. Their black and white stripes stand out starkly against the yellowish grassland, and you wonder how they evolved to look so conspicuous. Aren't prey animals supposed to blend into the background? Some of them look up as you pass by, but they don't seem bothered by you.

Go to page 30.

Zebra

- Zebra only live in Africa, and there are three different kinds: plains zebra, Grévy's zebra and mountain zebra. The ones you can see are plains zebra, which are the most common kind.
- Although a zebra's stripes make it stand out to us, the markings probably help with camouflage, confusing predators as to how far away the animals are. This makes it difficult for them to pick out one individual animal from a herd. The stripes might also deter biting insects, and help the zebra to recognise one another. No two zebras' stripes are exactly alike.
- Zebra live in family groups of one male and up to six females and their young. However, groups can join together to form huge herds.
- Although they're very similar to horses, zebra aren't used for riding or pulling carts because they're too panicky. There have been exceptions though – for example, in the 1800s, New Zealander George Grey imported zebra from Africa and used them to pull his carriage.
- Zebra aren't as fast as horses, but do have better stamina. Their excellent eyesight helps them to look out for predators.

You take a deep breath. The snake looks as though it could strike at any moment. You slowly take a step back. Then another. Finally you turn and run as fast as you can.

After a minute or so you risk a look behind you – the snake is nowhere to be seen. You stop running, and bend over, panting. You watch the ground carefully for any sign of movement. The snake has definitely gone.

In fact, the snake was a black mamba, one of Africa's most deadly snakes. Find out more about them on page 27.

Go to page 24.

After you've been walking for a while, you notice something at the edge of your vision. You stop and scan the tall grass. What you see freezes you to the spot. It's a rhinoceros.

You would have been delighted to see a rhino if you were with your group on safari. Black rhinos are an endangered species, and this is one of the few places in the world where you stand a good chance of seeing one. But alone, with no vehicle to protect you or help you get away, it's a very different story. These animals are enormous, armed with large horns, and have a reputation for being grumpy.

What should you do to avoid making the rhino charge? Should you stand your ground, or creep away slowly and carefully and hope that it hasn't seen you?

If you decide to stay where you are and stand your ground, go to page 31.

If you decide to try and get away without it seeing you, go to page 35.

You walk around the swamp, and as you get onto firmer ground you feel a bit more confident. In fact there aren't any crocodiles in the Ngorongoro Crater, but there are hippos, and they can be just as dangerous.

As you walk through a small wood you hear a loud groaning sound. Your heart pounds. What can be making that noise? As you come through the trees and onto dry grassland you get your answer: a herd of grazing wildebeest. There must be hundreds of these odd-looking animals scattered across the crater floor. You hope the animals aren't dangerous – they look quite fierce, with their long, bearded faces and sharp horns. You also hope there aren't any predators stalking them.

Go to page 21.

Wildebeest

- Wildebeest means 'wild beast' (not surprisingly) in Afrikaans. They get their name because of their strange, menacing looks.
- They are a type of antelope, and are also known as gnus. Despite their appearance, wildebeest aren't dangerous.
- Wildebeest are some of the largest antelope: they can measure 2.5 metres long, stand 1.5 metres at the shoulder, and weigh up to 300 kilograms.
- Every year, about 1.5 million wildebeest migrate across the Serengeti in Tanzania, usually in May or June, in search of better grazing. Hundreds of thousands of other animals, including zebra and different kinds of antelope, join the migration.

Ahead of you, the sun glints on sparkling water. You suppose it must be a swamp or a water hole – there's plenty of fresh water in the Ngorongoro Crater, which is why it's such a haven for wild animals. But as you draw closer, you realise it's much bigger. This must be the lake you've heard about in the crater, Lake Magadi. Pink flamingos crowd one edge of the lake. It's a beautiful sight.

It might be a good idea to fill your water bottle from the lake. On the other hand, it might be a better idea to concentrate on finding rescue – there are plenty of dangerous wild animals here in the crater, and you're likely to encounter one of them before you die of thirst.

If you decide to carry on in your original direction away from the lake, go to page 17.

If you decide to go to the lake, go to page 46.

Flamingos

- Both greater and lesser flamingos come to feed in the Ngorongoro Crater. They leave the crater at night.
- Flamingos are often hunted by jackals and hyenas around the lake edge.
- Greater flamingos are large birds – they stand up to about 130 centimetres tall, with a wingspan of over a metre and a half. Lesser flamingos are smaller, about two thirds of the size of greater flamingos.
- Flamingos' famous pink colouring is due to the soda-loving algae they eat. If they don't eat the algae, they become much paler.
- The birds use their webbed feet to stir up shallow water, then they submerge their large, bent bills to suck up mud, algae, and tiny creatures – their bills filter food out of the mud and water.

The snake is a black mamba, one of Africa's deadliest snakes. You've heard of black mambas before, and know that they are venomous and can be aggressive. You tell yourself that this snake can't be a black mamba because of its colour. Actually it's the black inside the snake's mouth that gives it its name. Unfortunately, you're about to see it.

The snake is even more alarmed now that you're encroaching on its territory. It raises the front of its body entirely off the ground so that its head is about level with your chest. A flap like a cobra's appears behind its head, and it starts to hiss. You shout and wave your arms and hope that this will scare it away. Unfortunately this prompts the snake to strike at you several times, delivering a fatal amount of venom in its bite.

You lay on the ground, in deep shock. It's only a few moments before the powerful toxins get to work, and it's all over within less than an hour.

The end.

Black Mamba

- Black mambas are some of the most feared snakes in Africa. They can be very aggressive if they feel threatened, and their venom is deadly. They are responsible for human deaths every year, though not nearly as many as the puff adder.
- Black mambas are one of the world's fastest snakes – they can travel at 20 kilometres an hour, without the benefit of legs!
- The black mamba is Africa's longest venomous snake: they can grow to more than four metres long, though on average they measure around 2.5 metres. They can raise up to half their body length off the ground.
- The snake's name comes from the black inside of its mouth, which it displays when it feels threatened.
- There is an antivenom available, but if you are bitten by a black mamba and don't receive treatment you will almost certainly die.

You're running at full pelt, but you can hear the rhino charging along, hot on your heels, making the ground shake. You can hear its snorting breath close behind you. You realise it's just a matter of time before the enormous beast catches up with you.

It only takes another couple of seconds for the creature to reach you. The rhino hits you at an astonishing speed, hurtling into you with the force of a truck. You die immediately.

The end.

Black Rhinoceros

- Both black and white rhinoceroses are found only in Africa, and both are actually grey in colour. The difference between them is in the shape of their lips – black rhinos have pointed upper lips while a white rhino's upper lip is square.
- Rhinos have a very good sense of smell and hearing, but their eyesight is very poor. If you had stepped behind a tree, or climbed up out of its line of vision, the rhino would probably have left you alone.
- These powerful animals can measure up to 1.8 metres at the shoulder, and weigh 1400 kilograms – that's as much as a family car!
- Black rhinos have two horns on their heads. The longer front horn can be 1.5 metres long! In some cultures the horn is used as medicine, and rhinos continue to be killed for this reason, even though rhino horn isn't actually an effective medicine at all.
- A baby rhino stays with its mother until it's about three years old. After that it leads a very solitary life.
- Rhinos feed mainly at night or during twilight. During the day they spend most of their time lying in the shade, or wallowing in mud pools.
- Other types of rhino – found in South Asia – are the Indian, Sumatran, and Javan rhinoceroses.

The most straightforward route to the edge of the crater looks like it's through a swamp. However, you're pretty sure you can see a clear way through it.

What kind of animals live in swamps here in Tanzania? Could there be crocodiles? Maybe you should go around the swamp instead?

If you decide to avoid the swamp, go to page 22.

If you decide to go through it, go to page 51.

The rhino turns towards you, sniffing the air. It does not look happy. It backs up a bit, and for a few seconds you think it must have decided to go away. But then it snorts, paws the ground, and begins to charge towards you.

There's a tree nearby. Should you climb it? Even if you do manage to get up into its branches in time, you worry that the rhino might keep you trapped up there for ages. You know that the rhino can outrun you, but you've heard that you can confuse rhinos by running in a zigzag, and they often give up the chase. Whatever you decide, do it quickly!

If you decide to run in a zigzag, go to page 28.

If you decide to run to the tree and climb it, go to page 40.

You realise with horror that you've come too close to these huge birds. One of them stares at you, fluffs up its feathers, and stalks towards you. You decide that the only option is to raise your arms above your head to make yourself look bigger. Hopefully this will frighten it off. You've read that ostriches aren't very clever.

Unfortunately, this makes no difference at all. If anything, it makes the situation worse. The ostrich squawks, and runs towards you in a feathery flurry with its wings outstretched. You bolt away as fast as you can, but the ostrich can run much faster than you. It catches up with you, kicks out with its feet, and you are killed instantly by the long, sharp claws on the ostrich's feet.

The end.

Ostriches

- Ostriches are the world's biggest birds. They can measure up to 2.7 metres tall (which is probably about a metre taller than an adult man) and weigh up to 160 kilograms.
- They live in grasslands and deserts in many African countries.
- Ostriches don't need to drink as they get all the water they need from the plants they eat. They also eat insects and lizards.
- The birds can sprint up to 70 kilometres per hour, and cover up to five metres in just one stride.
- Ostriches live in small herds of ten or so.
- Their giant eggs are the largest in the world – they weigh as much as 24 chicken eggs!
- Ostriches' claws are long and sharp, and they've been known to kill lions in self defence.
- Ostriches are farmed for their meat. They kill a few people every year, and most deaths occur on ostrich farms. They can be especially aggressive when they are with their young.

You're sure you made the right decision about that plant. Even, though water would be a priority in a normal survival situation, you're so vulnerable to animal attack that it has to take second place.

In fact you were right to be wary of the plant – it's very poisonous (see page 81).

You carry on, noticing that the ground is becoming damp and swampy.

Go to page 62.

You start to walk away, very slowly, keeping your eyes fixed on the rhino. The animal sniffs the air, and then looks away from you. You take the opportunity to move a bit more quickly. The rhino turns to look at you again, and you freeze.

After a few agonising moments, the huge animal seems to lose interest, snorts a bit, and then starts chomping on the grass again. Phew. But you don't feel completely out of danger until you've put some more distance between you and the rhino.

Black rhinos can be aggressive when they feel threatened, more so than white rhinos, so you were right to be cautious. To find out more about rhinos, turn to page 29.

Go to page 14.

The hippo turns towards you and opens its cavernous mouth. Perhaps it's just yawning, you think. It's not. It's giving you a strong warning that if you come any closer, it will attack you.

The hippo breaks into a run, heading straight for you. You start to back away, but it's too late. Coming between a hippo and its route to water is very dangerous. The hippo soon catches up with you, and takes a massive bite with its enormous tusk-like tooth. It's over very quickly.

The end.

Hippopotamuses

- Hippos are huge. They can be 1.5 metres tall at the shoulder, 3.5 metres long, and weigh more than three tonnes.
- Hippos spend most of their time in water – their eyes and nostrils are near the top of their heads, so they can breathe and see while they're almost completely submerged. They're good swimmers and can hold their breath for up to five minutes.
- Hippos come out of the water to eat grass. If they're disturbed or feel threatened on land they head straight to water. If you're blocking a hippo's path to water, or to its young, it's likely to become very cross.
- It's unwise to make a hippo angry because they can be extremely aggressive. They also have massive teeth – up to 70 centimetres long – and have been known to bite crocodiles in half.
- Hippos are considered to be some of the most dangerous animals in Africa. If you see one, keep your distance, don't make any loud noises or threatening movements, and get ready to back off very quickly!

The animal is moving towards you. It holds its head up high, snorting and looking very threatening. As it gets closer you can see that it's absolutely massive. The sun glints on its sharp horns.

Maybe there's still a chance you can get away? Perhaps you should hide behind a tree?

If you decide to hide, go to page 60.

If you decide to ignore the buffalo and hope it'll get bored, go to page 42.

As you walk away from the gazelle you begin to have the strange feeling that you are being watched. You keep walking and try to ignore it.

Something in the long grass ahead of you catches your eye. A prickle of fear runs down your spine as you peer into the tall, yellow grass. Suddenly, the reason for your fear becomes very clear. At the edge of the long grass, barely visible, is a large female lion. She's completely motionless, and watching your every move intently.

Your instinct is to run away screaming. You try to control your panic. What should you do? You've heard that making yourself look bigger can make predatory animals back off. But maybe that would only make things worse?

If you decide to stand still, go to page 113.

If you decide to make yourself look bigger, go to page 13.

You grab the lower branches of the tree, thankful that this isn't one of the many African plants with vicious thorns, as the great beast hurtles towards you. Seconds after you've swung yourself up into the branches, the rhino powers into the tree trunk. The whole tree shakes, and for a moment you worry that it's going to fall over. Thank goodness the tree took the brunt of the rhino's charge, and not you!

The rhino snorts and shakes its head. It sniffs the air, perhaps sensing that you're nearby. You feel like whimpering with fear, but manage to control yourself. Eventually the animal gives up, and wanders off to graze elsewhere. You wait for a while until it's at a safe distance, then climb carefully down from the tree and continue on your way.

In this situation, it's more important for you to get out of the way of dangerous wild animals than to keep yourself hydrated. Rescue is possible within a few hours, so you shouldn't be in danger of dying of thirst.

Water holes can easily become contaminated by animal waste, and unfortunately for you that's the case with this one. You soon start to feel sick, and have to lie down. In your weakened state it's only a matter of time before you're attacked by a pack of opportunistic hyenas.

The end.

You close your eyes tight, hoping that when you open them again the enormous, lumbering beast will have stopped moving towards you. You risk a peek – it's still there and it looks even bigger than ever. Maybe you should have climbed that tree after all.

Suddenly the animal puts its head down and charges. It gores you with its huge horns, and you're knocked unconscious as you fall to the ground and bleed to death.

The end.

Cape Buffalo

- Cape buffalo are the biggest member of the antelope family: large males can measure up to 3.5 metres long, 1.8 metres at the shoulder, and weigh a tonne.
- The horns can measure more than a metre across in larger animals.
- Female Cape buffalo and their young live in herds of up to a thousand. Male Cape buffalo tend to live alone. The animals are very protective of their calves and of one another.
- Cape buffalo are fierce and even lions run away from their massive horns. They can and do attack people. One of the worst times to approach them is during the hottest part of the day, when they usually rest and don't like to be disturbed.

You take off, sprinting faster than you ever have before. But you should have realised that predatory animals instinctively chase animals that are running – that's what they expect their prey to do.

Your blood runs cold as you hear the lion's low roar. It only takes a few seconds before the powerful creature catches up with you, brings you to the ground with its powerful claws, and delivers a deadly bite to the back of your neck.

The end.

Lions

- Lions live in groups, known as prides. They are the only type of cat to do so. Prides include up to three male lions, ten or more female lions (also called lionesses), and their young.
- Female lions are the main hunters of the group. They use teamwork to bring down prey animals that can run faster than they can, but they also hunt alone, and steal kills from smaller predators.
- Male lions, with their huge shaggy manes, can weigh up to 200 kilograms, and measure two metres long. In the Ngorongoro Crater there are lions with impressive black manes.
- Male lions defend the pride by marking their territory with urine, and roaring impressively to intimidate would-be intruders.
- As well as the lions that live in Africa, there is one group of lions that lives in Asia, in Gir Forest in India.
- Lion attacks on people are rare. If a lion ever confronts you, don't run away. Instead, try to make yourself look bigger (by holding a jacket up over your head, standing with legs wide, etc.), and talk firmly and calmly. This will help you to avoid looking like prey. Never turn your back on a lion.

As you get closer to the lake, you realise that what you thought was water around the edges of the lake are actually white salt deposits. Closer to the centre of the lake, the flamingos stand sieving the salty water through their bills.

This is an alkaline lake (or 'soda' lake), so the water isn't drinkable. The water is also warmed by hot springs, and you know that warm water is more likely to have bacteria in it than cold, fresh water. You won't be filling your water bottle here.

Go to page 17.

Lake Magadi

- Also known as Lake Makat, Lake Magadi is near the centre of the Ngorongoro Crater. Its size varies according to the season. At the height of the dry season there might be no water at all, just a salt plain.
- The lake's high concentration of salts includes the kind you put on your chips as well as other minerals. Because of its salt content, there aren't any fish in the lake.
- On one edge of the crater are stone burial mounds, which are thought to have been left by the Datoga people in the 19th century, before they were driven out by the Maasai. Datoga people still live in Tanzania.
- There are other sources of water in the crater, for example Ngoitokitok Spring, near the crater wall, and other small springs, which provide water for animals all year round, even during times of drought.

You pick up the bottle and turn it upside down, but the scorpion stays put. It's a fairly small, brown scorpion with a thick, yellow-coloured tail. It doesn't look particularly dangerous.

You shake the bottle a few times but the scorpion seems determined to stay inside. You give the bottle one last shake, and at last the creature flies out . . . on to your arm! You shriek as the scorpion stings you once, then again as you try to knock it off with your hand.

The stings are very painful. You know that most scorpions in Tanzania aren't dangerous, and you hope that the sting will be like a bee sting – painful, but not life-threatening. But it's not long before you start to feel groggy, and have to sit down. You feel weak and ill. The scorpion's venom isn't enough to kill you, even though it's stung you twice. But it is enough to make you sick and unable to move. A pack of spotted hyenas finds you shortly afterwards. (To find out more about hyenas, turn to page 75.)

The end.

Scorpions

- The scorpion you've just encountered is a member of the species Parabuthus. Most kinds are not considered to be especially dangerous, though there's one type that lives in southern Africa that has been known to kill people.

- Other Tanzanian scorpions to look out for are the Tanzanian red clawed scorpion, and the red bark scorpion, both of which can give you a nasty nip, though they probably won't kill you.

- The two most dangerous scorpions in the world are fat-tail scorpions and deathstalkers. Fat-tails live in north and west Africa, as well as the Middle East, Pakistan, and India, and cause a number of human deaths every year.

- Deathstalkers live in North Africa and the Middle East. They're highly venomous, but even so a healthy adult human being wouldn't usually die from its sting.

One of the shapes detaches itself from the trees. It's an ostrich! It looks as though there are a few more, but you can't tell how many because of the trees.

You're walking straight towards them. You'll soon find out how many there are. But maybe you shouldn't go near them? It would mean going out of your way a bit though as the birds are right in your path to the crater's edge.

If you decide to keep away from the birds, go to page 61.

If you decide to keep going as you are, go to page 32.

You're pretty confident that there aren't any crocodiles here in the Ngorongoro Crater, and in fact you're right. At least that's one large, meat-eating animal you can cross off your list of things to worry about.

But as you walk on the increasingly damp ground, you begin to notice animal tracks in the mud. They look quite big. There are probably easier routes to take than this. Maybe you should change direction to get away from the swamp?

If you decide to change direction, go to page 16.

If you decide to keep going, go to page 12.

The snake has made you nervous, even though it wasn't interested in you. As well as scanning the grassland for predators, you'll have to keep an eye on the ground in front of you, too.

Go to page 72.

Hyenas are dangerous animals, so you were right to keep well away.

There are some trees in the middle distance, straight ahead of you, and you think you caught sight of a movement close to them. You're immediately alert. You carry on walking, watching the trees intently.

Go to page 50.

You spot a large plant – almost a tree – with branches that look very much like a cactus's. You've heard that you can drink the sap of cactus and other succulent plants. In fact people have survived on moisture from cactus plants when there's no other form of drinkable water available. You snap off a piece of the plant, and sure enough there is a white liquid inside it.

Should you drink some of the liquid, or carry on feeling thirsty and in danger of dehydration?

If you decide to drink the sap, go to page 80.

If you decide to carry on, go to page 34.

Ngorongoro Crater Plant Life

- The most common type of plant on the crater floor is grass. There are lots of different kinds, and some of the taller ones are pretty and colourful.
- In the rainy season colourful flowers sprout on the grasslands and crater rim, where mosses and ferns also grow.
- The swampy areas of the crater are full of sedge, reeds and grasses.
- There are different types of euphorbia plant in the crater, especially on the crater rim. They protect themselves with spines and poisonous sap.
- The trees of the wooded areas in the crater are mostly yellow-barked acacia, which is also known as the fever tree because it often grows near water where malaria-carrying mosquitoes breed.
- Strangler fig trees smother other types of tree until they completely overwhelm them and stand on their own with huge, trailing roots reaching to the ground.
- The Sodom apple plant bears round, yellow fruit, which are poisonous.
- Definitely don't eat any fruit you see!

The snake coils into an S-shape. Then it lunges at you, biting you deeply on the arm. You pull your arm away, horrified, and clamber back down the tree as quickly as you can.

The bite is painful. You tear off a strip of your shirt and tie it firmly around the bite. Then you carry on walking, assuming that the snake either wasn't venomous, or didn't deliver its venom when it bit you (it's quite common for a venomous snake not to inject poison when it bites).

However, in a couple of hours you start to feel very sick. Your head pounds, you feel nauseous, and start to become confused. You slump to the ground in the shade of a tree, and fall unconscious. You don't wake up.

The end.

Boomslang

- Boomslangs vary in colour depending on whether they're male or female. The one that's just bitten you is a male, and is pale green in colour. Females are usually brown.
- They look different from most other snakes because of the size of their eyes, which are large and round – boomslangs have very good eyesight.
- The snakes can grow up to about 1.8 metres long, though usually they're about a metre or a metre and a half long.
- The boomslang's venom is very powerful, and acts by stopping blood from clotting. However, they don't kill very many people because they're quite shy creatures.
- Boomslangs are only found in Africa south of the Sahara desert.

You walk on, glad that you decided to avoid the fierce looking buffalo. In fact, Cape buffalo can be very aggressive (turn to page 43 to find out more about them).

There's a movement up ahead of you and you strain your eyes to try and make out what it might be. You follow the swish of a long, thin, spotted tail . . . it's a cheetah! It's moving stealthily, with its back to you. Maybe it's stalking a gazelle.

You don't think that cheetahs attack people – but you're not sure. Although it's smaller than the lions you've seen, probably less than half the size, it's still a powerful animal with sharp teeth and claws. Maybe you should climb a tree? Or should you just stay still and wait for the animal to move away?

If you decide to climb a tree, go to page 102.

If you decide to remain still and wait, go to page 90.

Cheetah

- The cheetah is the smallest of the big cats. It weighs up to 65 kilograms.
- Cheetahs are famous for being the fastest land animals in the world. They can accelerate from zero to 100 kilometres an hour in about three seconds, which is faster than most cars!
- The animal's top speed, sprinting in short bursts, is around 120 kilometres an hour. Its long tail helps it balance as it zooms along.
- Cheetahs hunt during the day. Camouflaged by their spotted coats amongst tall grass, they creep as close to their prey as they can before beginning a sprint to bring it down.
- Cheetahs' main prey are gazelle, smaller antelope, young zebra, wildebeest, hares, wild sheep and other smaller mammals.
- There are fewer than 10,000 cheetahs in the wild, mostly in eastern and southwestern Africa.
- Cheetahs are unlikely to attack people, but they are still dangerous wild animals and might attack if they feel threatened.
- If you do feel as if a cheetah might attack, climb a tree: cheetahs very seldom climb trees, and have trouble getting down again if they do.

You duck behind a tree, and press your back up against it, facing away from the buffalo. Your fingers dig into the bark and you close your eyes, hoping that the animal won't come looking for you.

After ten minutes, you risk a look behind the tree. You can still see the buffalo, but it's lumbering off in the opposite direction. You let out a long breath of relief.

Go to page 58.

You spot a group of gazelle, and see that they're drinking at the edge of a small pond. You have hardly any water left in your bottle and you're thirsty. You know that dehydration can kill. Should you fill up your bottle from the water hole?

If you decide to drink from the water hole, go to page 41.

If you decide not to, go to page 73.

There are so many animals concentrated into a small area in the Ngorongoro Crater that you soon spot a different kind: a group of monkeys. They're fairly small, with grey bodies and cute black faces surrounded by fluffy white fur. They turn to look at you curiously as you pass, and two of the monkeys come running towards you for a closer look.

You watch the monkeys watching you as you pass by. Then suddenly one of them makes a high-pitched chattering noise. More of them join in, and they lose interest in you completely. They stand up and start studying the ground.

The monkeys are clearly alarmed. Should you be too? Should you go and investigate?

If you decide to find out what the monkeys are making all the fuss about, go to page 76.

If you decide not to, go to page 72.

Vervet Monkeys

- Vervet monkeys are fairly small animals, up to about 50 centimetres long with greyish bodies and black faces.
- Vervets live in many different countries throughout Africa, and also on several different islands in the Caribbean, where they arrived on ships from Africa in the 1600s.
- They're mostly vegetarian, but sometimes they also eat insects, eggs, and even small rodents or baby birds.
- Vervets live in groups of up to about 70 animals.
- They communicate with different calls, and even have different calls for specific predators. They have distinct calls to warn of leopards, eagles, pythons and baboons, which are the animals most likely to attack them.

Most predators are likely to chase you if you run – that's what their prey do, so their instinct is to run after you. And most big predators will be much faster than you.

The leopard takes a huge bound as you start to run, and it's only a few more seconds before the animal leaps on top of you, pins you to the ground, and bites through the back of your head, killing you instantly.

The end.

Leopards

- Leopards live in northeast Africa, Africa south of the Sahara desert, and also in central Asia, India and China.
- These big cats are extremely powerful. Their bodies measure up to about two metres long, and can weigh up to 80 kilograms.
- They are excellent climbers, and often drag their prey up into trees after a kill, where it's safe from scavenging hyenas and other animals.
- Apart from mothers and their cubs, which stay with the mother leopard for about two years, leopards are usually solitary animals.
- Leopards have distinctive black spots to help camouflage them from their prey, but in some leopards the spots are joined up so that the animal's fur is almost completely black. These leopards are often known as black panthers.

You leave the bottle by the boulder and carry on. You feel bad about littering the crater with the plastic bottle, but you really didn't like the look of that scorpion.

You spot another group of vervet monkeys by some trees. As you pass by, one or two of them start making a low-pitched grunting sound, and more of the monkeys join in.

The monkeys must be warning one another that a predator is close. They're looking upwards, and running off to hide in bushes and trees. What should you do?

If you decide to climb a tree, go to page 110.

If you decide to hide behind a boulder, go to page 89.

The jackals don't seem to have noticed you – maybe the wind is blowing in the wrong direction for them to pick up your scent, or maybe they're too intent on the carcass that they're eating. You give them a wide berth anyway. You can't be too careful.

You're right to be cautious, but in fact jackals aren't usually a danger to people and would probably run away if you approached them (turn to page 101 to find out more about jackals).

Go to page 93.

Here in the Ngorongoro Crater, the large numbers of gazelle, wildebeest, zebra, and other prey animals attract various different predators. You spot a hyena loping through the grass towards the herd of gazelle.

The hyena seems intent on a young gazelle, which is standing slightly apart from the rest of the herd. Should you be worried about the presence of the hyena?

If you decide not to worry and carry on in your chosen direction towards the crater's edge, go to page 86.

If you decide to walk in the opposite direction from the gazelle and the hyena, go to page 53.

Thomson's Gazelle

- Gazelle are a type of antelope, and there are lots of different kinds, including Thomson's gazelle, the animal you can see, and Grant's gazelle, which are also found in the Ngorongoro Crater.
- Thomson's gazelle can be up to about 80 centimetres tall at the shoulder and weigh up to 75 kilograms. Grant's gazelle are slightly bigger.
- The gazelle live in herds that can contain hundreds of animals.
- Predators of gazelle include cheetahs, hyenas, lions, and leopards. They can run very fast to escape them – up to 65 kilometres an hour. Thomson's gazelle also make huge, long leaps, known as 'pronking'.

Baboons are large, intelligent animals with powerful jaws full of sharp teeth. They can be dangerous to people.

The big male baboon rushes up to you and tries to take your backpack. You remember that there's an apple in the bottom of the bag, and he can probably smell it. You pull the backpack away from him, but he shrieks and attacks, giving you a horrible, deep bite on your leg. Then he rushes off with your backpack.

You are in severe pain and bleeding freely from the wound in your leg. You sink to the ground, and eventually pass out. You don't wake up.

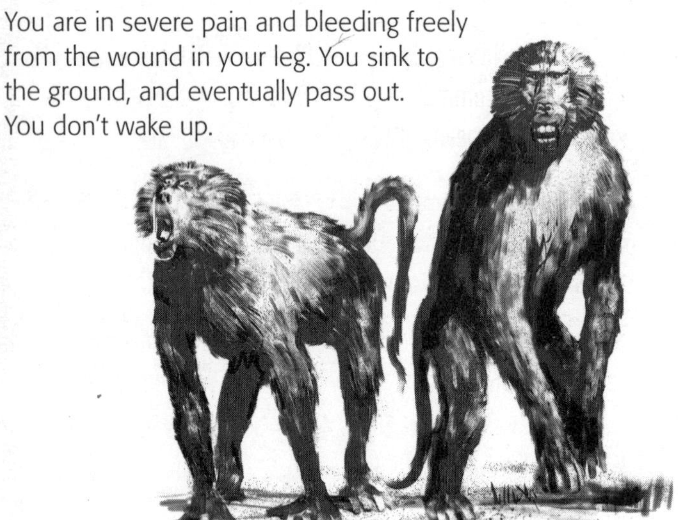

The end.

Baboons

- Baboons are some of the largest monkeys in the world, and can grow up to a metre tall.
- They eat grass, fruit, seeds, and other vegetation, and they also eat meat – mainly birds and rodents, but sometimes they kill the young of sheep and gazelle.
- Baboons live in large groups and have a complicated social system. They communicate with a variety of different calls with different meanings.
- There are five different kinds of baboon, all of which live in Africa or the Middle East. The ones you've just encountered are olive baboons.
- Baboons have been known to hurt people, but you were extremely unlucky to be killed. They don't see people as prey, but they can be aggressive, especially if food is involved.

You don't see any more monkeys as you continue on your way, but you do spot a much bigger animal – a large, lone, bull-like creature with horns, which you recognise as a Cape buffalo.

The animal turns and looks your way. You're not very close, so it must have caught your scent on the breeze. Should you back off and avoid the buffalo? Or should you keep going?

If you decide to keep going, go to page 38.

If you decide to avoid the animal, go to page 58.

You're feeling thirsty, hot and tired. You thought you might have seen a jeep with tourists on safari by now, but you've been unlucky. There are so many dangerous animals about that you can only hope to find help soon.

Go to page 54.

You decide to try and make yourself look bigger, so you stretch your shirt across your arms and hold it above your head. One of the hyenas notices your sudden movements and turns to look at you. You wave your arms and shout.

Now you've got the attention of all the hyenas in the pack. They spread out around you, and one of them runs at you, knocking you to the ground. The others join in the attack. It's a messy and painful way to go, but at least it's over fairly quickly.

The end.

Spotted Hyenas

- Spotted hyenas are the largest species of hyena – they can weigh up to 80 kilograms and measure 1.5 metres long.
- Hyenas are pack hunters, and can prey on animals as large as wildebeest (see page 23). They also scavenge food.
- They have sharp hearing and keen eyesight. They are also fast runners with lots of stamina.
- Many people think hyenas are a type of dog, but in fact they're more closely related to cats.
- Spotted hyenas are famous for their 'laugh' – it's one of the various sounds they make to communicate with one another.
- Hyenas have powerful jaws that can crunch bones. The animals can even digest teeth!
- Hyenas do attack and kill people – beware!

The monkeys are still making the chattering noise and staring at the ground. You go over to see what they're making all the fuss about, but you can't see anything. You scan the damp ground . . . and suddenly you see it: a massive snake, thicker than your arm.

The snake is a rock python, a constricting snake that sometimes preys on vervet monkeys. The noise the monkeys are making is their special alarm call for a snake. You carefully step out of the snake's way, as it slithers along the ground. It's not interested in you – it's searching for a small animal to squeeze to death.

Go to page 52.

Rock Python

- Rock pythons are Africa's largest snake and can be as long as six metres. They prefer wetter areas.
- They are constricting snakes and they aren't venomous. Instead of using venom, they squeeze their prey to death in their powerful coils.
- Rock pythons can eat animals the size of antelope! Specially hinged jaws allow them to swallow their prey whole.
- Rock pythons have been known to kill people, but it's very rare.

Very slowly and carefully, you back away from the leopard and make your way towards a tree a few metres behind you. The leopard's gaze is still fixed on the trees where the monkeys are. You slip behind a tree and wait. It seems to take forever, but eventually the leopard gives up and slinks off.

Heaving a sigh of relief, you continue your jouney to the crater's edge. In the distance you spot a magnificent sight: elephants. There are several animals in the group, some of them babies. They lumber along, grabbing grass and leaves with their trunks. One of them, a huge male with long tusks, has large wet patches behind his eyes. He's flapping his ears and charging about. You're still quite far away from the animals. What should you do?

If you decide to climb a tree, go to page 82.

If you decide to get away as quickly and quietly as possible, go to page 94.

African Elephants

- African elephants are the world's largest land animal. They can reach six tonnes in weight and measure four metres at the shoulder.
- These enormous animals need a lot of food to keep them going. They can eat 135 kilograms of food a day. Their diet includes grass, leaves, roots, fruit, and bark. They spend most of their time foraging for food.
- Elephants' trunks have thousands of muscles and are used for grasping food, picking up water or dust for a bath, or comforting young.
- Both male and female African elephants have tusks, which they use for digging and to strip bark from trees. Male elephants also use the tusks to fight one another.
- Elephants have been killed for their ivory tusks, which is very valuable. Today it's illegal to do this, but, sadly, it still happens.
- Female elephants live in family groups with their young, while male elephants tend to roam about on their own.
- Elephants can be dangerous to people – see page 83.

What on earth were you thinking? You should never eat a plant in the wild unless you're absolutely sure what it is. And as it turns out, this one is poisonous.

The sap, or latex, tastes very bitter on your tongue, which you should take as a warning sign. However, you're convinced that you've read about this plant and its bitter taste, and that it's good for you. It's true that the plant's latex is sometimes used as medicine, but not without diluting it first. It's also true that the undiluted latex is sometimes used to tip poisoned arrows.

Your tongue starts to blister and soon you're in terrible pain. You start to vomit as your body tries to rid itself of the poison. It's not long before it kills you.

The end.

Euphorbia Candelabrum

- There are 2000 species of euphorbia, some of which are popular garden plants all around the world. This one is a grey-barked tree up to 12 metres tall with fleshy branches that contain a lot of latex.
- In Africa, the latex is sometimes used to treat medical conditions. Small amounts are mixed with water or food and used to treat various illnesses such as stomach aches, or to make patients sick if they've eaten something poisonous. It can also be applied to wounds to help them heal.
- The latex is also used to tip arrows with poison for hunting.
- The plants produce yellow flowers that are rich in nectar, but the honey produced from it isn't good to eat because it makes a burning sensation in the mouth.

The elephant is in musth, which only happens to male elephants, and makes the animals produce a chemical that shows up as wet patches on their faces. No one knows exactly why it happens. Elephants in musth become extremely aggressive. They have been known to gore rhinos, and chase vehicles, digging their tusks into the ground in frustration when they can't catch up. In zoos, elephants in musth have to be isolated, and have killed zoo keepers in the past.

Your position up a tree doesn't save you. Once the elephant catches your scent on the wind, he's after you. He attacks the tree with his tusks, knocks it over completely, and tramples you into the ground.

The end.

Elephant Attacks

- Elephants are the world's largest vegetarians. But even though they don't attack other animals for food, they can be ferocious when they're defending themselves or their young, or when they're fighting over food.
- As you've just discovered, male elephants are especially dangerous when they're in musth, when they become very aggressive.
- African elephants are losing their habitats as cities, towns, and farmlands spread out. This means that elephants are coming into contact with people more than ever before. Some researchers think they're becoming more aggressive because of this.
- People on safari have been attacked – see page 120 – and elephants are so large that a vehicle doesn't necessarily put them off.
- Far more elephants are killed by people than the other way around. About a thousand elephants per year are killed for their ivory tusks, or because they've become a nuisance to people.

You spot an enormous cow-like animal with two long, twisted horns. It's reddish brown, with white stripes down its body. You haven't seen one of these animals before. Although the creature looks quite docile, and doesn't seem at all bothered by you, you still feel nervous. After all, it is huge, and those horns look sharp!

The animal raises its head and looks at you, then goes back to grazing on the grass. As quietly as possible you retreat further back away from the animal, and then get away from it as quickly as you can.

Go to page 103.

Giant Eland

- The animal is a giant eland, the world's largest antelope. Large males can measure 1.8 metres at the shoulder, and weigh up to a tonne.
- Elands usually live in herds of up to about 25 animals. They eat grass, leaves, and other plant material, and mostly feed at night.
- Giant elands can move surprisingly fast despite their size. They can run at 70 kilometres an hour, and jump 1.5 metres high.
- Although their large, spiral horns look dangerous, giant elands aren't aggressive to people. They use their horns to break off tree branches, for self-defence, and male elands use them in fights to compete for females.
- Predators of the giant eland include lions and spotted hyenas, and sometimes leopards prey on young, old or sick animals. Because of their size, they're not easy prey.

You carry on walking, keeping an eye on the hyena. Soon another hyena appears, and then another.

Now you're worried. Hyenas are pack animals, and act together to bring down their prey. They're interested in the gazelle, not you, but you should probably do something to make sure they don't attack you. Maybe you should shout at them and shoo them away? Or is it better just to avoid them as best you can?

If you decide to shout at the hyenas, go to page 74.

If you decide to walk in the opposite direction, go to page 53.

The monkeys are running up into the trees, scampering up the trunks to the very highest branches, still making their short, harsh cries of alarm. You look around – what could be worrying them? Maybe it's a snake or a scorpion?

It's something much bigger. With a horrible shock, you suddenly make out the spotted coat of a leopard, camouflaged amongst the grass. It's watching the last few monkeys clambering nimbly into the trees.

Go to page 92.

You wait to make sure the cheetah has gone. Then you carefully edge along the branch, away from the snake, moving as slowly as you can so as not to alarm it. The snake watches you with its surprisingly large eyes, but doesn't move. Without making any sudden movements, and keeping an eye on the snake, you climb down from the tree, then run to a safe distance.

You were right to be concerned about this snake – it's a deadly boomslang (find out more on page 57).

Go to page 106.

You run towards a boulder and crouch behind it in the shade. The monkeys are scampering into bushes and up trees, where they huddle in the middle of the branches. You're wondering if you should climb up after them since they're all up in the trees and you're on the ground. But they do seem to be looking upwards.

You shade your eyes from the sun and scan the blue sky.

Go to page 96.

You stand very still. The cheetah hasn't taken any notice of you. Instead, it's focusing intently on the little antelope. It crouches down low, its eyes trained on its victim. Then it creeps towards the antelope stealthily, drawing closer and closer.

Suddenly it powers out of the long grass at lightning speed. The dik-diks stampede.

You hold your breath as you watch the fast, frantic chase, the targeted dik-dik leaping and zig-zagging with the cheetah hot on its hooves. But the dik-dik manages to out-manoeuvre the big cat, and bounds away into the undergrowth following the rest of its herd.

The cheetah lies panting in the grass, exhausted from its high-speed sprint. You move off cautiously, making sure you don't attract its attention – you'd be nowhere near as fast as a dik-dik.

Go to page 106.

Dik-dik

- Dik-diks are small antelope, only about 40 centimetres tall at the shoulder and just six kilograms in weight.
- They get their unusual name from the female dik-dik's alarm call. Both female and male dik-diks also make a whistling noise that's thought to be a warning to other animals that there might be predators about.
- Female dik-diks are bigger than males, but to make up for it male dik-diks have short horns.
- Dik-diks don't usually live in herds like other antelope. Instead, breeding pairs have territories that they mark with scent glands in the corner of their eyes.

You can hardly believe your eyes. It's unusual to see a leopard, partly because they usually hunt at night. But this one is definitely on the prowl now. Its large, yellowish-green eyes are fixed on the monkeys. It licks its lips as it looks up into the trees, ready to spring.

Even though the leopard is stalking the monkeys rather than you, your heart is pounding wildly. The monkeys have cleverly made for the smallest branches at the top of the tree, which won't support the leopard's weight – or yours. What should you do?

If you decide to run, go to page 64.

If you decide to stay where you are, go to page 99.

You're feeling a bit more confident with every step that brings you closer to the edge of the crater.

After a while, you spot a group of baboons scattered in front of you. They're sitting around calmly, grooming one another, and eating. They turn to look at you as you get closer. They have long snouts, like a big dog's muzzle, but they don't look threatening.

The baboons are in your way. You don't want to have to walk around them and make your route across the crater any longer than it needs to be. But maybe you should. Are baboons aggressive?

If you decide not to alter your route, go to page 109.

If you decide to give the animals a wide berth, go to page 105.

You realise that the elephant is in musth – you've read about this in your guidebook and know that it is a condition that no one completely understands, but results in male elephants becoming extremely aggressive. Keeping an eye on the elephants, you swiftly put as much distance as possible between you and them in as short a time as possible. You can only hope that the male elephant doesn't spot you or catch your scent because if he does he'll almost certainly attack.

You break into a jog through a small wooded area. You feel much safer once you're on the other side and out of the elephants' line of vision. You were right to get away as quickly as you could.

You slow to a walk, watching as a fox-like animal with enormous ears stares at the ground in front of it. The animal is so intent on what it's doing that it doesn't notice you at all. Suddenly it pounces, digging under the sandy ground, and runs off munching a fat grub.

Go to page 111.

Bat-eared Fox

- The animal you've spotted is a bat-eared fox. Its ears, which can measure up to 15 centimetres tall, look far too big for its head. As well as giving the fox keen hearing, the ears are full of blood vessels that lose heat and help keep the fox cool.
- Apart from their ears, bat-eared foxes are small. They are about 40 centimetres at the shoulder and weigh up to about 4.5 kilograms.
- Bat-eared foxes are found in eastern and southern Africa. They live in underground dens, which have several entrances and chambers connected by tunnels.
- The foxes aren't big enough to prey on mammals - they eat insects, grubs, and worms instead.
- Their hearing is so good that they can hear insects or insect larvae moving underneath the ground. They listen to work out where the unseen creature is, then quickly dig it up and eat it.
- Bat-eared foxes have to watch out for cheetahs, leopards, hyenas, eagles, and rock pythons, which all prey on them.

Finally you spot what the monkeys seem to be worried about. You make out the dark shape of a bird of prey. As it swoops down, its claws outstretched, you see that it's an eagle. But the monkeys have cleverly positioned themselves deep within the tree branches, making it very hard for the eagle to get at them. The eagle misses out on a meal and the vervets are safe, thanks to their clever alarm calls. The eagle flies away, thwarted.

You continue on your way. Ahead of you there's a stretch of long grass. Should you find a way around it, or walk through the long grass?

If you decide to walk through the grass, go to page 108.

If you decide not to, go to page 103.

Martial Eagle

- The eagle preying on the monkeys was a martial eagle, a large, dark brown eagle with a white breast.
- These birds are the biggest eagles in Africa: they can grow to be nearly a metre long from the beak to the tail, with a wingspan of nearly two metres, and weigh up to seven kilograms.
- The martial eagle eats a wide variety of different prey, including birds, lizards, snakes, and mammals such as monkeys, hares, and young antelope.
- The eagle lives throughout Africa south of the Sahara Desert, but their numbers are in decline, partly because they are killed by farmers worried about their livestock.

You finish your water and put the bottle down next to you, then shade your eyes to try and judge the distance to the crater's edge. You're about to pick up the bottle again, but jerk your hand away – a scorpion has just crawled into the bottle!

It's not that far to the edge of the crater and you could probably make it without a bottle of water. But there might be valuable water sources between here and there where you could refill your bottle and have another drink. You feel quite thirsty even now. On the other hand, is it worth getting the scorpion out of the bottle, and most likely annoying it in the process?

If you decide to remove the scorpion from the bottle, go to page 48.

If you decide to leave the bottle, go to page 66.

The leopard is looking up at the monkeys on the top-most branches of the tree. Maybe the big cat can see that they're too high up for her to go.

A sweat breaks out on your forehead that has nothing to do with the heat of the day. Standing where you are, you're completely exposed. It's only a matter of time before the powerful leopard realises that you're there, and that you're probably easier to catch than the monkeys. What should you do?

If you decide to climb a tree, go to page 104.

If you decide to hide behind a tree and wait, go to page 78.

As you draw closer to the jackals they look up from their gory meal to look at you. One of them runs off, blood dripping from its mouth. Two jackals remain around the carcass, but they don't seem to be bothered by you. You make sure you don't get too close to their food, and carry on your way.

Go to page 93.

Golden Jackals

- There are three species of jackal that live in Africa: the common or golden jackal, the side-striped jackal, and the black-backed jackal. The one you've just seen is the golden jackal, which is the biggest kind at about one metre long and half a metre to the shoulder.
- Jackals usually hunt alone or in pairs, although sometimes bigger family groups hunt in packs, and if there's some tasty carrion to scavenge a big group of jackals might congregate around it.
- Jackals prey on rodents, small mammals, birds, lizards, snakes, fruit, and insects. They aren't usually dangerous to people.
- Jackals usually hunt at dawn and dusk to avoid the hottest part of the day.
- Golden jackals also live in Asia, Europe and the Middle East.

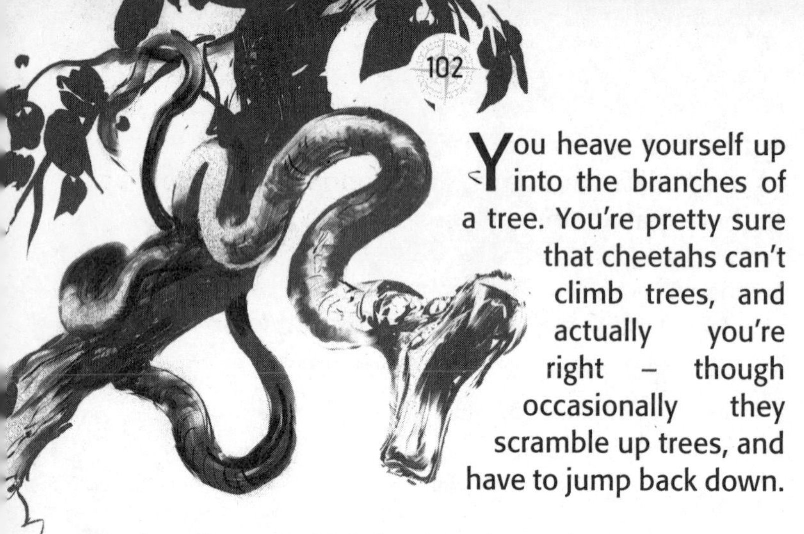

You heave yourself up into the branches of a tree. You're pretty sure that cheetahs can't climb trees, and actually you're right – though occasionally they scramble up trees, and have to jump back down.

You're so busy watching the cheetah crouching in the long grass that it takes you a while to spot a much closer threat: coiled on a branch next to you is a long, green snake. Its scales glisten in the sun and it is looking at you with unusually large (for a snake) black eyes. You freeze in terror. What should you do?

You know that there are lots of venomous snakes in Africa. But is this one of them? Perhaps you should climb back down from the tree slowly? You check, and see that the cheetah has moved off, so you don't need to worry about that. But moving might give the snake a good chance of striking at you. Maybe it would be better to knock it off the tree quickly with your foot.

If you decide to kick the snake off the tree, go to page 56.

If you decide to climb down, go to page 88.

You find a way around the long grass instead of through it. You were worried about animals lurking in there that you might not spot until it's too late.

You haven't gone very far when the vervet monkeys pipe up again, this time with a series of short, harsh cries. You have no idea what it means, but there are plenty of dangerous predators about, and some of them could be just as threatening to you as to the vervets.

Should you stop and find out what the danger is? Or should you keep going?

If you decide to stop, go to page 87.

If you decide to keep going, go to page 112.

Still facing the leopard, you edge slowly towards the tree a few metres to your right. A few quick strides later and you're swinging yourself up into its branches.

Unfortunately, so is the leopard. And it's a much better climber than you are. It drags you down with its powerful claws and delivers a quick, sharp bite to your skull, killing you instantly. (To find out more about leopards, turn to page 65.)

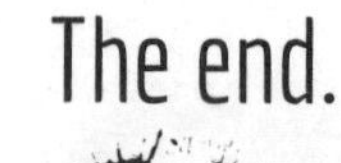

You walk backwards, keeping your eyes fixed firmly on the baboons. The bigger ones look intimidating and powerful, and they don't seem to like the look of you at all. Maybe they're worried about the babies in the group, or maybe they're just territorial.

Once you've backed off for ten metres or so, the baboons stop showing their teeth and staring at you. While a couple are still watching you, they don't seem so interested any more.

You were right to back away from them. These animals can be very dangerous. (Turn to page 71 for more information about them.)

Go to page 114.

You walk for a while, but the hot sun is beating down on you and you decide to rest in the shade for a moment and get your breath back. You spot a big boulder that casts a small shadow, and go and sit down near it to drink the last of your water.

Go to page 98.

Ngorongoro Crater Climate

- There is a wet season and a dry season in this part of Africa. In Ngorongoro, most of the rain falls in the wet season, from November to May.
- The amount of rain per year varies a lot, but on average the crater floor gets about 700 millimetres of rain per year, the eastern forested slopes of the crater about 800-1400 millimetres, and the western slopes of the crater get about 400-600 millimetres.
- Temperatures vary too - the coldest months are June and July, when it can be surprisingly cold, especially higher up on the rim of the crater.
- The crater's permanent springs and swamps mean that there is water in the crater even in the driest months, between June and October.

Your encounter with the eagle makes you more aware of birds. There are various kinds of birds of prey here, as well as vultures. They don't seem big and scary enough to attack a human being … but you never know.

The long grass swishes as you walk through it. It comes up to your shoulders, so you can still clearly see where you're going.

As you get closer to the group of baboons, you start to feel threatened. One of them – a big male – runs towards you and stops about ten feet away, making what sounds like a threatening call and showing his teeth. He has very long, sharp fangs.

You worry that a confrontation is unavoidable. If you back off, will the baboons see that as a weakness and attack? If you keep going, will that just antagonise them more? What should you do?

If you decide to keep going and tough it out, go to page 70.

If you decide to back off and change your route to the crater's edge, go to page 105.

It's not long before you see what the monkeys are making all the fuss about: a huge bird of prey is in the sky, and it's circling the trees that the monkeys are in. It looks like an eagle, brown in colour with a white chest. You don't think the bird would harm you, but you never know – you remember hearing about a wildlife cameraman who was attacked by an eagle.

You sit in the tree branches and wait.

Go to page 96.

You're hot and thirsty. Although you've seen plenty of wildlife, there's a particular species you're hoping to see but haven't so far: human beings. You still haven't spotted a jeep full of tourists, or any of the Maasai people who live here. Shouldn't your tour group be looking for you by now?

You carry on walking. A growling, snapping sound alerts you to the presence of a group of jackals not far away. They seem to be fighting over the carcass of a small antelope. Are they dangerous? Should you avoid them?

If you decide to keep clear of the jackals, go to page 67.

If you decide they're not dangerous, go to page 100.

As you walk, you think you catch sight of something in the long grass. But when you stop and look, you can't see anything there. You keep going, feeling more and more nervous. You squint into the grass as you carry along your way. Finally you start to make out a shape. You squint harder, slowing your steps. It's a spotted big cat – a leopard.

If you decide to run away, go to page 64.

If you decide to stop and stand still, go to page 99.

The lion stays exactly where it is, crouched in the yellow grass. You are beginning to shake with fear, and realise that your policy of standing still and hoping for the best doesn't seem to be working.

To your alarm, the lion takes a tentative, very slow step towards you, still in its crouching position. It looks ready to spring.

You're going to have to do something. Should you run away? Or try making yourself look bigger, perhaps by using your shirt?

If you decide to run away, go to page 44.

If you decide to make yourself look bigger, go to page 13.

You're nearing the crater's edge now, but you still can't see any signs of human habitation. A soft tinkling sound reaches you on the breeze, and you stop and strain your ears . . . it's the sound of a bell! You remember that the cows the Maasai people keep wear bells around their necks! You break into a run and head towards the sound. Sure enough, on the other side of a small wood, you see probably the most welcoming sight of your life: a group of Maasai tribespeople and their herd of cattle!

You're safe at last. The people give you a drink and help you to the nearest campsite, where you make contact with your tour group. Soon you're back at the campsite where you're staying, telling everyone about your dangerous day alone and on foot in the Ngorongoro Crater. Your African adventure is over.

The end.

Maasai Cattle

- Cattle are very important to the Maasai people: they rely on them for food, use their dung to make houses, wash clothes and hands with their urine, and make clothes, bedding, sandals, and ropes from their skins.
- The Maasai's cows are called zebu. They have horns and a big hump on their back.
- It's quite rare for a cow to be killed for its meat. This only happens on special occasions.
- The Maasai people drink the cows' milk and also their blood. To do this, a cow is pierced with an arrow to let some blood out, then the wound is sealed. People drink the blood on its own, mixed with milk, or made into a special dish.
- Each cow in a herd has a different-sounding bell so that individual cows can be identified from the sound.
- The cows sometimes become prey to lions, leopards, and hyenas. They're brought inside village compounds at night, which are surrounded by thorny branches, to protect them from predators.

African Countries

How many African countries can you name? Here is an alphabetical list of all of them. Test yourself on how many you already know before you look at it.

Algeria, Angola, Benin, Botswana, Burkina Faso, Burundi, Cameroon, Cape Verde, Central African Republic, Chad, Comoros, Democratic Republic of the Congo, Djibouti, Egypt, Equatorial Guinea, Eritrea, Ethiopia, Gabon, Gambia, Ghana, Guinea, Guinea-Bissau, Ivory Coast, Kenya, Lesotho, Liberia, Libya, Madagascar, Malawi, Mali, Mauritania, Mauritius, Morocco, Mozambique, Namibia, Niger, Nigeria, Republic of Congo, Rwanda, São Tomé and Príncipe, Senegal, Seychelles, Sierra Leone, Somalia, South Africa, South Sudan, Sudan, Swaziland, Tanzania, Togo, Tunisia, Uganda, Zambia, Zimbabwe

The People of the Ngorongoro

Most of the people who live in the Ngorongoro Conservation Area today are Maasai tribespeople. In the past, they lived inside the Ngorongoro Crater, but now the government of Tanzania only allows them to graze their cattle there during the day.

Maasai were famous as fierce warriors, and until the European settlers arrived in Europe they had won the most fertile lands in their part of Africa for themselves. At the beginning of the twentieth century, they lost most of their land to the Europeans. Today's Maasai warriors still wear traditional red robes, carry spears, and wear their hair in braids covered in ochre.

The Maasai society is centred on their cattle (see page 115) and other animals. Wealth is measured by how many cows people own. But life is gradually changing: instead of a traditional nomadic lifestyle herding cattle, building temporary homes as they move, lots of Maasai have settled in permanent villages, and more and more of them are choosing to work in tourism, or to go and live in cities. To earn extra money, the Maasai who live in the Ngorongoro area often pose for tourists' photographs, or sell hand-made jewellery and ornaments.

Ancient Ancestors

Our human ancestors have lived in the area around the Ngorongoro Crater for millions of years.

In the Olduvai Gorge, a ravine 50 kilometres long and up to 150 metres deep, fossils have been found of some of the oldest human-like creatures ever found. During the 1930s, fragments of a 1.75-million-year-old skull were found, similar in some ways to modern humans', which was nicknamed Nutcracker Man because of his powerful jaws.

Forty kilometres south of Olduvai, in 1974 the skeleton of 'Lucy' was found – a female of the species called *Australopithecus afarensis*, more than three million years old, and the most complete human-ancestor skeleton ever found up until that time. In 1979 fossilised footprints were discovered that had been left in wet volcanic ash in the same area. They belonged to two human-like adults and a child, who had walked there around 3.75 million years ago.

Tanzania's Top Spots for Tourists

As well as the beautiful Ngorongoro Crater and the area around it, Tanzania is also home to other incredible sights . . .

Mount Kilimanjaro

This is the biggest mountain in Africa, at nearly six kilometres high. At the base of the mountain is a tropical jungle, but its peak is covered in snow all year round. People come from all over the world to climb Mount Kilimanjaro, which takes about a week.

The Serengeti

The Serengeti, which adjoins the Ngorongoro Conservation Area, is a vast area of grassland, forests, and swamps, and one of Africa's most famous national parks. Every year millions of wildebeest, zebra, and antelope migrate 800 kilometres across the Serengeti, preyed on by predators including lions, hyenas, and crocodiles. In the Maasai language, Serengeti means 'endless plains'.

The Great Rift Valley

This spectacular valley cuts through Tanzania for 6,600 kilometres from north to south. It was formed 20 to 30 million years ago by the movement of the tectonic plates in the Earth's crust. The valley is up to 70 kilometres wide, and in places its floor is a kilometre beneath the surrounding plains.

Lake Tanganyika

In western Tanzania, this is the world's longest freshwater lake, at 677 kilometres long. It's also the world's second deepest lake (after Lake Baikal in Siberia) at 1,436 metres deep, and Africa's second largest lake (after Lake Victoria). It was formed during the upheaval of the Earth's tectonic plates that formed the Rift Valley. The lake borders Burundi, Zambia, and the Democratic Republic of Congo, as well as Tanzania.

True Tales

People really have ended up lost in the African wilderness. Here are just a few of these frightening true-life stories.

In 2009, American tourist **Tom Siebel** set off on a walking safari in the Serengeti with a guide. By a watering hole, the two men avoided a herd of buffalo, then spotted a herd of elephants about 200 metres away from them. A large female elephant turned towards them, outstretched her ears, trumpeted loudly, and charged at the men. First she picked up the guide with her trunk and flung him aside. Then she knocked Siebel to the ground, rolled him over, trampled him and injured his leg with her tusk. When the elephant finally retreated, Siebel was left alive but very badly hurt. The guide wasn't badly hurt and raised the alarm, and Siebel was taken to hospital. His injuries included six broken ribs, an injured shoulder, and a badly broken leg, which needed sixteen different operations.

In January 2014, a British teacher, **Sarah Brooks**, was on holiday with her fiancé in Kruger National Park, South Africa, when they were attacked by a bull elephant. The elephant was in musth (see page 82) and turned and attacked the small hire car that Brooks was driving. In her panic, Brooks couldn't find the reverse gear to get away. The elephant overturned the car, smashed the windscreen, and gored Brooks' leg with his tusk, before walking away. Brooks' fiancé wasn't hurt and raised the alarm. Brooks recovered in hospital.

In 2003, South African holiday-maker **Diana Tilden-Davis** was canoeing in the Okavango swamp in Botswana, when she accidentally bumped into a hippo. The animal attacked and bit through her leg. Tilden-Davis survived the attack, but earlier in the same month another woman was killed by a hippo. It's thought that the animals were more stressed than usual because of a drought.

Glossary

antagonise – annoy or irritate

congregate – gather in a crowd

conspicuous – very easy to see

crater – a large, basin-shaped land feature

dehydration – suffering from a lack of water

docile – gentle or easy to control

gores – stabs with a horn or tusk

gory – covered in blood

grooming – animals cleaning each other

haven – safe place

hydrated – having enough water in your body

impending – about to happen

instinctively – acting on instinct (natural ability, knowledge or usual behaviour)

intimidate – frighten

ivory – the material elephant tusks are made of

latex – the milky sap of some plants, used to make rubber

malaria – a serious disease, carried by mosquitoes

musth – a time when male elephants are very aggressive

nomadic – not having a permanent home but moving from one place to another

opportunistic – taking advantage of what is available

out-manouevre – make a clever move to escape something

plains – broad expanses of flat lands

ravine – a land feature with steep sides and a stream running through it, like a valley or canyon but smaller

scavenging – feeding on dead animals that other animals have killed

smother – suffocate, cover up so air can't get to something

stamina – the strength to carry on doing something for a long time

stampede – when a large group of animals charges at once because they're excited or frightened

succulent – juicy, water-storing

tectonic plates – huge sections of the Earth's crust, which push against each other or pull away from each other

territories – areas claimed and defended by particular animals

venomous – capable of injecting venom

Index

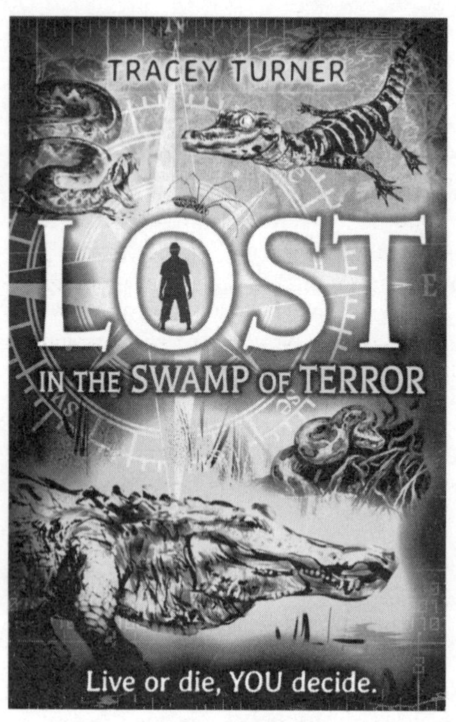

Lost... In the Swamp of Terror

You've survived the terrifying creatures of the Ngorongoro Crater, but have you got what it takes to survive the unpredictable Everglades swamp? From powerful alligators to deadly rattlesnakes, can you make it out alive?

Live or die – you decide.

£4.99 ISBN 978-1-4729-1541-2

Extract from Lost... In the Swamp of Terror

Suddenly you're in the middle of one of your worst nightmares: you've walked straight into a huge spider's web! The cobweb clings to your face and shoulders. You shut your eyes tight and desperately claw the web off you – when part of it moves! You open your eyes to see a large spider with a long body squirming in the web, right on your face!

You scream as you brush the web and the spider off you. The creature scuttles off into the leaves on the forest floor. You hope it hasn't bitten you and that the spider isn't venomous if it has.

After that horrible experience, maybe you should get out of this forest?

If you decide to carry on as you are, go to page 107.

If you decide to find a way out of the forest, go to page 77.

EAST SUSSEX COU
WITHDR
-8 JUL 2024
24